WORLD'S WORST FAMILY?

Adapted by Farrah McDoogle
Illustrated by Andrew Ross

Ready-to-Read

Simon Spotlight
New York   London   Toronto   Sydney   New Delhi

SIMON SPOTLIGHT
An imprint of Simon & Schuster Children's Publishing Division
1230 Avenue of the Americas, New York, New York 10020
This Simon Spotlight edition September 2020
TM & © 2020 Sony Pictures Animation Inc.
All Rights Reserved.
FURBY ® & © 2020 Hasbro, Inc. Used with permission.
All rights reserved, including the right of reproduction in whole or in part in any form.
SIMON SPOTLIGHT, READY-TO-READ, and colophon are registered trademarks of Simon & Schuster, Inc.
For information about special discounts for bulk purchases, please contact Simon & Schuster Special
Sales at 1-866-506-1949 or business@simonandschuster.com.
Manufactured in the United States of America 0720 LAK
2 4 6 8 10 9 7 5 3 1
ISBN 978-1-5344-7343-0 (hc)
ISBN 978-1-5344-7342-3 (pbk)
ISBN 978-1-5344-7344-7 (eBook)

It all happened so fast.
The robots tried to take over
our planet, but they lost the
battle in a few days.
This is the story of what happened,
and the special family who saved
the world.

To understand what happened,
you need to meet the Mitchell family.
Before the robots took over,
the Mitchells did not seem
like heroes.

The Mitchells were just an average family.
They were the last family anyone would ever expect to help save the world from robots!

The dad, Rick Mitchell,
loved nature.
A lot!
The Mitchell kids couldn't
understand how anyone could
love nature that much.

The mom, Linda Mitchell,
was a proud mother with a big heart.
She was happy when her family
was happy.

The daughter, Katie Mitchell,
couldn't wait to leave for college.
She loved movies.
She wanted to make films.
She wished her dad understood her.

The son, Aaron Mitchell,
loved dinosaurs.
He also loved his dog, Monchi, and
his big sister, Katie.
He was going to miss her when she
left for college.

Aaron wasn't the only Mitchell
who loved Monchi.
All the Mitchells loved their pet dog.
That was one of the only things they
could all agree on!

Now that you know what
the Mitchells were like
before the robot takeover,
let's see what happened
during the robot takeover.

How did the robots do it?
A computer assistant named PAL
took control of everything
with a computer chip in it, including
the new line of PAL Max robots.
The humans panicked!
They did not know what to do
without their devices.

The robots tricked the humans. They said the humans would love spending time in human fun pods. By the time the humans realized that the pods were not fun at all, they were trapped inside!

Some humans tried to fight back,
but it did not work.
Soon everyone on Earth was
captured, except for the Mitchells.

"We're the last people left,"
Katie said.
"Everything will be fine. I have a
plan," said Rick.

Rick wanted to get rid of all their electronics and stay put to stay safe.

Katie wanted to dress up as robots
to try to trick the real robots.
Then she wanted to use a kill code.
A kill code would make it so the
robots would not work.
Rick said Katie had watched
too many movies.

Katie and Rick could not agree
on a plan.
"Stop!" Linda said.
Then she asked what a regular
family would do.

Katie did not care about that.
"Rick Mitchell taught me to be bold
and never play it safe," Katie said.
Her dad listened.
The Mitchell family decided
it was time to take some risks.

The Mitchells met two robots,
Eric and Deborahbot 5000.
The robots were damaged during
the takeover and did not work
correctly. They accidentally told
Katie how to upload the kill code.

To do it the Mitchells needed to get to the mall.

The mall had a PAL Labs store. They could upload the kill code there, but getting to the mall would be dangerous!

"The highway is crawling with robots," Rick said.

Katie had a plan to hide their car!
They covered the car with a cloth
so it would look like the road.
They tricked the robots!
"Amazing!" cheered Rick.

They reached the mall safely,
but PAL knew they were coming.
PAL controlled the robots and all
the electronics with an Internet
connection, so every device
attacked the Mitchells!

It seemed like no place in the mall was safe.

"Grab anything without a chip,"
Rick exclaimed.
Katie found fishing rods!
The Mitchells could use those to
fight back!

Next the Mitchells ran to a toy store.
The Furbies attacked them,
but the Mitchells did not give up.
It looked like the Mitchells might
win until . . .

The leader of the Furbies joined the fight!

"I will avenge my fallen children!" it shouted.

"Why would someone build that?" Katie asked.

Eric the robot was stuck under a pillar during the battle. Linda saved him!

Katie was almost finished uploading
the kill code, but the Mitchells
were trapped.
Rick knew what to do!
"Grab the lights!" Rick yelled.
Together the Mitchells pulled on
a strand of lights and brought down
the leader of the Furbies.

PAL saw what happened at the mall.
She flew into a rage and screamed,
"Send in the stealthbots!"
PAL could not understand how the
humans could be winning.
PAL did not think the Mitchells
were anything to worry about.
PAL was wrong!

The Mitchells dressed up as robots
to fool the stealthbots.
This time the stealthbots
were not fooled.
But the Mitchells did not give up.
They were brave!
They were heroes!

The Mitchells might be average in many ways, but after the robots tried to take over, they are above average at loving each other. Together they saved the world!